CALENDAR CLUB MYSTERIES

The Case of the
APRIL FOOL'S
FROGS

by **NANCY STAR**

Illustrated by
JAMES BERNARDIN

SCHOLASTIC INC.

New York   Toronto   London   Auckland   Sydney
Mexico City   New Delhi   Hong Kong   Buenos Aires

To Rebecca, Ben, and Sammy
—N.S.

To all the kids in Ms. Lertora's kindergarten
class at Wilkes Elementary School.
—J.B.

ISBN 0-439-67266-X

Text copyright © 2006 by Nancy Star
Illustrations copyright © 2006 by Scholastic Inc.
All rights reserved. Published by Scholastic Inc.

SCHOLASTIC and associated logos are trademarks
and/or registered trademarks of Scholastic Inc.

12 11 10 9 8 7 6 5 4 3 2   6 7 8 9 10 11/0

Printed in the U.S.A.
First printing, April 2006

Book design by Jennifer Rinaldi Windau

CHAPTER ONE
GOWKS!

Dottie noticed it first.

"Look!" she said. "A poster!"

She pointed at the big oak tree in front of Fruitvale Elementary School.

A large poster was attached to the tree.

"What does it say?" asked Casey.

"Let's go find out," said Leon.

Dottie Plum, Casey Calendar, and Leon Spector were best friends and next-door neighbors.

They were also the first and only members of the Calendar Club. And the Calendar Club loved to find things out.

They hurried to the tree.

Leon read the poster out loud.

FIRST-EVER FRUITVALE
APRIL FOOL'S DAY
FESTIVAL!

Place: Fruitvale Park
Time: Noon
First Event: Look-alike contest!
Winner gets a Gowk!

"What's a gowk?" asked Casey.

"Maybe it's a kind of owl," said Leon. "It's sort of spelled like the word 'owl.'"

Dottie took a small notebook out of her back pocket. She carried her notebook wherever she went. Inside she kept lists. Her favorite list was of the weather.

Today, Dottie's weather list said, is seventy degrees and sunny.

Dottie started a new list. She called it: What's a Gowk?

She wrote down Leon's idea: Could be a kind of owl

"You two should enter the look-alike contest," Leon told his friends. "Then you can win a gowk and we can find out what it is."

"But we don't look alike," said Dottie.

"What if I carry a notebook wherever I go?" asked Casey. "What if I write down everything everyone says? Then, people might think I'm you."

"I could wear my hair in braids," Dottie said. "I could ask a million questions."

Casey was famous for asking lots of questions.

"I think you'd win a gowk for sure," said Leon.

"But what is a gowk?" asked Casey.

"Maybe it's a kind of cat," said Dottie.

Dottie had a cat named Ginger who

thought she was a dog. Ginger loved to go for long walks on a leash.

"Maybe it's a kind of dog," said Casey.

Casey's dog, Silky, thought he was a cat. He liked to sit at the window and watch the world go by.

"It's definitely not a kind of rock," said Leon.

Leon couldn't have a pet because of allergies. So he collected rocks shaped like states instead. His goal was to find enough rocks to make an entire map of the United States.

"Maybe Mr. Cliff knows what a gowk is," said Dottie.

Mr. Cliff owned Pet Me, a pet store in Fruitvale. And he knew a lot about animals.

"We can go to town and ask him," said Leon.

"Did you forget?" said Casey. "We can't go to town now. A new family moved in on

Red Rose Lane. And my mom left a tray of brownies on my kitchen table for us to bring over to them."

Mrs. Calendar owned Sweetie Pie, the bakery next door to Pet Me. She made welcome brownies whenever people moved to Fruitvale. Dottie, Casey, and Leon thought Mrs. Calendar's brownies were the best in the world.

"I didn't forget," said Leon. "I've been thinking about those brownies all day."

"We can go see Mr. Cliff after we deliver the brownies," said Dottie.

Her friends agreed. They hurried on their way.

They were halfway to Daisy Lane when Leon stopped.

"Look," he said. "Another poster."

A girl and her mom were standing in front of it, reading what it said.

The three friends walked over.

"Hi," Casey said to the girl.

"Hi," said the girl.

Casey read the poster aloud.

"FIRST-EVER FRUITVALE APRIL FOOL'S FESTIVAL!

SECOND EVENT: EGG-JUGGLING CONTEST!

FIRST-TIME JUGGLERS ONLY!

LAST EVENT: IT'S A SURPRISE!

EVERY WINNER GETS A GOWK!"

"You should enter the egg-juggling contest," Dottie told Leon. "Then you can win a gowk, too."

"I don't know if I want a gowk," said Leon.

"Do you know what a gowk is?" Casey asked the girl. "Do you know what the last event is? Are you going to the April Fool's Festival tomorrow?"

The girl nodded. "I'm going," she said quietly.

"We are, too," said Dottie.

"We'll see you there tomorrow," said the girl's mom.

They waved and walked away.

"Let's stop by the clubhouse and check the Help Box," said Dottie.

"Then we can deliver the brownies and go see Mr. Cliff," said Leon.

The clubhouse was in Casey's backyard. The Help Box was where anyone in Fruitvale could put a note if they had a problem.

Dottie ran to the clubhouse so she could get there first.

Dottie loved to be first. Her friends didn't mind. They were used to it.

"There's a note!" Dottie said as soon as Leon and Casey caught up to her.

"There's a bunch of notes!" she added.

Dottie kept a tally in her notebook of whose turn it was to check the box each day. Today was her turn to check.

She opened the box and took out the note on top. She read it out loud.

"A gowk is missing!
Can you help look?
Gowks like to leave clues
under trees and in books.
Gowks are shy.
Don't call their names.
But one was seen on Red Rose Lane."

"Who signed it?" asked Casey.

"No one," said Dottie.

"Red Rose Lane is where the new people live," said Leon.

"We can look for the gowk on our way there," said Dottie.

"What else is in the Help Box?" asked Casey.

Dottie lifted out another note and a pile of flyers.

Dottie gave the flyers to Leon. Then she read the second note.

"Can you share these flyers with neighbors and friends?
That really could help bring this search to an end."

Leon looked at the flyers. "The flyers are all about the missing gowk," he said.

"Want to give out the flyers on our way to deliver the brownies?" asked Casey.

"Yes," Dottie said. "Wait," she added. "I hear something."

They all listened. They all heard it.

A strange noise was coming from inside the Help Box.

CHAPTER TWO
FROGS!

They leaned closer. The sound
was definitely coming from inside the box.

"I didn't notice anything under the
flyers," said Dottie.

"Maybe it's hiding," said Leon.

"What is it?" Casey asked. "Is it the
gowk? Should I look?"

Before anyone could answer, she lifted
the lid of the box.

Something jumped out. Leon grabbed it.

"It's a frog!" he said.

He held on to it. But it wasn't easy. The
frog wanted to jump away.

Dottie ran and got a bucket from Casey's
garage.

Leon put the frog inside.

"Is a gowk a kind of frog?" asked Casey.

"I've heard of horned frogs, bullfrogs, and tomato frogs," said Leon. "But I've never heard of a gowk frog."

"How did a frog get inside our Help Box, anyway?" asked Casey.

Just then they heard loud laughter coming from the street.

They ran to see who it was.

Warren Bunn and Derek Fleck were standing in front of Casey's house.

Warren was a boy in their grade who was a bully and proud of it. Derek Fleck was his best friend.

Warren looked at the bucket. "What's in there?" he asked.

"A frog," said Leon.

"We found it in our Help Box," said Dottie.

"Did you put it there?" asked Casey.

"Warren won't touch frogs," said Derek.

"I will, too," said Warren. He scowled at Derek. Then he looked at Leon. "Hey, Leon," said Warren. His eyes got wider. "Don't move. There's a giant bee behind you. And it's got a stinger the size of my arm."

Leon froze. But he didn't hear any buzzing. Slowly, he turned to look for the bee.

"April Fool's," said Warren. "Made you look."

"That wasn't funny," said Dottie.

"Can't you take an April Fool's joke?" asked Warren.

"Yes," said Leon. "Except it's not April Fool's Day until tomorrow."

"Hey, Warren," said Dottie. "Your little sister, Emma, is running down the block. And she looks really excited about something!"

"Nice try," said Warren. "But you're not going to make me look."

"Warren!" Emma called.

They all turned. Emma Bunn was running down the block. She held a white sun hat in front of her. When she got to Warren she dropped it on the ground.

"There's a frog in my hat," she announced.

"*Ribbit*," said the hat.

"So what?" asked Warren. He took a step back.

Emma bent down and looked into her hat. "How did it get in there?"

Mrs. Bunn walked toward them. "Emma, why is your hat on the ground?"

"Because someone put a frog in it," Emma explained.

"Warren," said Mrs. Bunn, with a warning in her voice.

"It wasn't me," Warren said.

"Warren won't touch frogs," said Emma. "He makes me touch them instead. He's allergic, remember?"

"He's not allergic," said Derek. "He's just afraid to get warts."

"I don't care about warts," said Warren. He got on his bike. "Are you coming or not?" he asked Derek.

The two boys rode off.

Emma took the frog out of her hat. It was a very big and slimy frog.

"Do you want it?" Emma asked the three friends.

"Sure," said Dottie.

"We'll keep it with ours," said Leon. "You can visit it any time you want."

"Okay," said Emma. She handed Dottie her frog.

Dottie put it in the bucket.

Leon handed Mrs. Bunn a flyer. "This is about the missing gowk."

"Do you know what a gowk is?" Casey asked.

"Is it a kind of mouse?" asked Mrs. Bunn.

"We don't really know," said Leon.

"All we know is one is missing," said Dottie. "The flyers were in our Help Box. We're giving them out so everyone can help look."

"Is it little?" asked Emma. "Could a gowk be a bug?"

"Maybe," said Dottie.

"Come on, Emma," said Mrs. Bunn. "We can look for it on our way home."

"Okay," said Emma. She checked the grass for gowks as small as bugs as they walked away.

"I'll get the brownies," said Casey. She ran inside her house.

"Frogs like having rocks and twigs to climb on," Leon told Dottie. "I'll go look for some to put in the bucket. And I'll get some leaves for them to hide under, too."

"I'll get a shoebox," Dottie said. "In case we find more clues. Or in case we find the gowk."

Dottie went inside for a shoebox. Leon wandered off to look for rocks, twigs, and leaves.

Dottie was the first one back. She took out her notebook and started two new lists.

She called the first list: Clues for a Missing Gowk.

She called the second list: Frogs in Surprising Places.

Leon returned and put some twigs, rocks, and leaves in the bucket.

Casey brought the tray of brownies in her red wagon.

Then Dottie, Casey, Leon, the wagon, the shoebox, the bucket, and the frogs set off for Red Rose Lane.

CHAPTER THREE
MORE FROGS!

They were halfway down Red Rose Lane when Leon saw something.

"Look," he said. "There's a book leaning against that tree."

They ran over to get a closer look.

"Didn't the note say gowks leave clues under trees and in books?" asked Casey.

"Yes," Dottie said. She lifted up the book. There was a piece of paper inside it.

"Is that another note?" Casey asked. She pulled it out of the book.

Leon picked up something else.

"What's that?" asked Casey. "A rock?"

"No," said Leon. "It's a feather."

"It's beautiful," said Dottie.

"Could it be from a gowk?" asked Casey.

"It's definitely a clue," said Dottie. She turned to the page in her notebook called: Clues for a Missing Gowk.

She wrote down: First Clue: Bright blue feather with pale yellow spots.

Casey read the new note out loud.

"A gowk is missing!
Can you help find it?
If you see a red rock,
look behind it.
Gowks are shy.
Don't call their names.
But one was seen on Fernwood Lane."

"Fernwood Lane is on the way to town," said Dottie.

"We can go there on our way to talk to Mr. Cliff," said Leon.

"Look," said Casey. She pointed to a

house. "That's where the new people live."

They walked to Thirteen Red Rose Lane. A girl was sitting on the front steps.

"I remember you," said Dottie. "You were with your mom looking at the poster for the April Fool's Festival."

"I'm Lizzy," said the girl. "Are you two going to enter the look-alike contest?"

Dottie and Casey smiled.

"Why?" asked Casey. "Do you think we look alike?"

"Leon thinks if we dress the same we really might win," added Dottie.

"Who's Leon?" asked Lizzy.

Dottie and Casey turned to introduce Leon. But he was nowhere to be seen.

This was nothing new. Sometimes Leon wandered away looking for rocks.

"Leon," called Dottie and Casey together.

Leon came running out from behind a bush.

"Sorry," he said. "I found another frog."

"I love frogs," said Lizzy.

The frog squirmed. Leon walked to the wagon. He put the frog in the bucket.

Lizzy walked to the wagon, too. "You know what I love even more than frogs? Brownies."

"You do?" said Casey. "That's great. Because my mom made these brownies for you." She handed over the tray.

"Her mom makes the best chocolate-chip brownies in the world," said Leon.

"Have you seen my mom's store?" asked Casey. "It's called Sweetie Pie."

"Yes," said Lizzy. "It's right near the new store that's opening tomorrow."

"I didn't know there was a new store," said Casey. "What's it called?"

"It's a secret," said Lizzy.

"Why?" asked Casey.

Lizzy shrugged.

"Do you want to come to town with us?" asked Casey.

"No, thanks," said Lizzy. "But thanks for the brownies."

She took the brownies and went inside her house.

Casey looked around. "Where did Leon go now?" she asked Dottie.

"Leon!" Dottie and Casey called together.

Leon didn't answer.

They turned the corner onto Fernwood Lane.

Leon was standing there, waiting. He had found something. And the big smile on his face meant it was something good.

CHAPTER FOUR

MORE CLUES!

Leon opened his hand. "I found the red rock," he said.

"The one mentioned in the note?" asked Casey.

"Yes," said Leon. "And there was something under it."

Leon put the rock in his pocket. He pulled out a note and read it.

"A gowk is missing!
Where could it be?
Some say a gowk's
favorite number is three.
Gowks are shy.

Don't call their names.
But one was seen on Cherry Lane."

"We'll pass Cherry Lane on the way to town," said Dottie.

"Let's go," said Casey.

"Wait," said Leon. "There's one more thing." He opened his other hand. "I found this under the note."

Dottie and Casey looked at the thin, white string in Leon's hand.

Casey touched it. It was as hard as wire. "What is it?" she asked.

"That's what Uncle Eddy puts on his rod when he takes me fishing," said Dottie.

"Could a gowk be a kind of fish?" asked Casey. She put the string in the shoebox.

Dottie added it to the list of "Clues for a Missing Gowk."

"It could be," said Leon. "But the blue

feather we found made me think it was a bird."

"Could it be a birdfish?" asked Casey.

"I've never heard of a birdfish," said Leon. "But I never heard of a gowk, either."

They continued down the block. They put flyers in the mailboxes of all the people they knew.

They gave one to Mrs. Miller, who was standing in front of her house.

"Thank you," said Mrs. Miller. But she didn't read it. She looked upset.

"Is everything okay?" asked Casey.

"Not really," said Mrs. Miller. "I took this sandbox out last night to clean it."

She pointed to the large, green plastic sandbox on her front lawn.

"My grandkids are coming, and they love sand," she explained.

Casey heard a noise. "What's that?" she asked.

"That's the problem," said Mrs. Miller. "I was about to fill up the sandbox when I heard that noise."

"Could there be a gowk in the sandbox?" asked Casey.

"A shout?" asked Mrs. Miller.

"A gowk," said Dottie.

"What's a gowk?" asked Mrs. Miller.

Leon took the blue feather out of the shoebox.

"We're not sure," he said. "But it might have feathers like this."

"Frogs don't have feathers," said Mrs. Miller.

"Frogs!" said Dottie. "We thought they were gowks!"

"I don't know anything about gowks," said Mrs. Miller. "But I do know my sandbox is filled with frogs."

Dottie, Casey, and Leon lifted up the lid to the sandbox and looked inside.

"There are six frogs," Dottie said.

"I cannot keep six frogs in my sandbox," said Mrs. Miller.

"We could bring them to Mr. Cliff," said Leon. "We're on our way to see him now." He looked in the wagon. "I think we need some more buckets, though."

"I think I've got a couple," said Mrs. Miller.

She went and got two more buckets. Casey put Mrs. Miller's frogs in the buckets. And they continued on their way.

"Did you find it yet?" a voice called out.

They turned. Warren Bunn and Derek Fleck were riding their bikes. They skidded to a stop.

"You don't have to bother looking for the gowk anymore," said Warren. He waved one of the flyers in the air. "I know all about it. And I'm going to be the one to find it."

"Yeah," said Derek. "We're going to find it."

Warren pointed at Leon's foot. "Hey, Leon," he said. "How did your shoelace get stuck on that slimy thing?"

Leon looked to see what his shoelace was stuck on.

"April Fool's," said Warren. "Made you look."

"It's not April Fool's Day yet," said Leon.

Warren and Derek rode off laughing. Warren laughed so hard his bike started to wobble. He rode into the curb and fell off.

"Are you okay?" Dottie called.

"I'm fine," Warren said.

He got back on his bike.

"Don't forget to wear your helmet," a voice called out.

Dottie, Casey, and Leon turned. Officer Gill was standing at the corner.

"Come on," said Casey. "I bet Officer Gill knows what a gowk is."

And the three friends ran over to ask him.

CHAPTER FIVE
TURNING INTO TOADS

Officer Gill was talking to a man.

"Meet the Calendar Club," Officer Gill said to the man. "They're my favorite detectives."

"This is Mr. Mac," Officer Gill told the three friends. "He owns the new store opening near Sweetie Pie."

"We heard about your store," said Dottie.

"What's it called?" asked Casey.

"That's a big secret," said Mr. Mac.

"Why?" asked Casey.

"You'll have to wait till tomorrow to find out," said Mr. Mac. "Are you coming to the April Fool's Festival?"

The three friends nodded.

"Great," said Mr. Mac. "I'll see you there." He turned to Officer Gill. "Thanks for all your help," he said.

"That's what I'm here for," said Officer Gill.

Mr. Mac hurried away.

"Solve any mysteries today?" Officer Gill asked the three friends.

"Not yet," said Dottie.

"Have you ever heard of a gowk?" asked Casey.

"A grouse?" asked Officer Gill.

"A gowk," said Dottie.

Officer Gill noticed the buckets in Casey's wagon. "Are those gowks?"

"No," said Leon. "Those are frogs."

"That's what I thought," said Officer Gill.

"We've got nine of them," said Dottie.

"That's a lot of frogs," said Officer Gill. "I got a lot of calls about frogs today. Frogs have been showing up in some very odd places."

"Where?" asked Casey.

Officer Gill took his notebook out of his back pocket.

Dottie took her notebook out of her back pocket.

Officer Gill read from his notebook. "Mrs. Foust found a frog in her shoe. Mr. Elder found a frog in the school."

Mr. Elder was the principal of Fruitvale Elementary School.

"Who would put a frog in the school?" asked Casey.

"I don't know," said Officer Gill. "Can you think of anyone?"

Casey and Dottie looked at each other. They had the same idea.

Leon knew what they were thinking. "It can't be Warren Bunn," he said. "He thinks frogs will give him warts."

"I know," said Officer Gill. "I had a long talk with Warren about pranks this morning. But I don't think he's behind this one."

"We'll let you know if we find out anything," said Dottie.

"Thanks," said Officer Gill. "And good luck finding your grouse."

"It's a gowk," said Dottie.

"What is a gowk?" asked Officer Gill.

"We think it's either an owl, or a fish, or a frog," said Leon.

"But it could be a bug," said Dottie.

"I'll keep my eyes open for one of those," said Officer Gill. "I'll see you at the festival tomorrow."

He waved good-bye.

Leon was waving back when he noticed something.

"Look," he said to his friends. He pointed to a nearby tree. "There's a box."

He walked over to the tree and picked up the box.

"The number three is painted on the lid," he said.

"Didn't the last clue say gowks like the number three?" asked Casey.

Dottie nodded.

Leon opened the box. He looked inside. "It's a tooth," he said.

"A gowk tooth?" Casey asked.

Dottie took a look. "It looks like the fang of a snake."

"Could a gowk be a snake?" asked Casey.

"There's a note here, too!" said Leon.

He took out the note and read it out loud.

"Gowks go to sleep early,
and so should you.
Tomorrow, there's a lot to do.
The gowk must be found,

or you'll be a toad.
Bring your clues to the festival
at Fruitvale Park Road.
Find the gowk and you'll get prizes galore.
Surprises supplied by your friends at the
store!"

"What store?" asked Casey.

"I don't understand the part about being a toad," said Leon.

Dottie looked into one of the buckets.

"Maybe these aren't frogs," she said. "Maybe they're toads."

"Do you think they were once people?" asked Casey. "Do you think they were people who looked for gowks and couldn't find them?"

"No," said Dottie. She stared at the frogs.

"That one does look a little sad, though," she said, pointing to one of them.

"That one looks kind of mad," Leon said, pointing to another.

"I think we better talk to Mr. Cliff," said Dottie.

They hurried to Pet Me to see what Mr. Cliff could tell them.

CHAPTER SIX

WRONG DOOR!

Dottie got to town first. She waited for her friends to catch up.

She tried to peek in the window of the new store. But it was covered with paper, so she couldn't see inside.

Casey and Leon joined her. Together, they walked to Pet Me.

But when they got to the door of the pet store, they stopped.

There was a sign on the door. Leon read it out loud. "PLEASE USE OTHER DOOR."

"What other door?" asked Casey.

"There is no other door," said Dottie.

Dottie peered through the window. "Mr.

Cliff is inside," she said. "I can see him talking to a customer."

Mr. Cliff noticed Dottie, Casey, and Leon standing outside his store.

He waved. He motioned for them to come in.

The three friends shook their heads.

Mr. Cliff came outside. "Is everything all right?" he asked.

"We can't figure out how to get in your store," said Dottie.

"What's wrong with using the door?" asked Mr. Cliff.

Leon pointed to the sign. Mr. Cliff read it.

"I didn't put that sign on my door," said Mr. Cliff. "But I'd like to know who did."

"Hey, Leon," someone called out.

They turned. It was Warren Bunn.

"There's a giant spider behind you," yelled Warren.

This time Leon didn't look.

Warren and Derek sat on their bikes and laughed.

Mr. Cliff walked over to them.

"Did you put that sign on my door, Warren?" asked Mr. Cliff.

Warren stopped laughing. "Yes," he said. "But it was just a joke."

"I'd like you to take it down now, please," said Mr. Cliff.

"Okay," said Warren. He took the sign down. "Sorry," he added quietly.

"Hey, Leon," Derek called out. "There's a big, hairy monster behind you."

"We're not doing that anymore," Warren said. He got on his bike and rode away as fast as he could.

Derek hopped on his bike and tried to catch up.

Dottie, Casey, and Leon followed Mr. Cliff into his store. They brought the buckets with them.

"What do you have in there?" asked Mr. Cliff.

"Frogs," said Leon. "Lots of frogs."

"Did you stop by to find out how to take care of them?" asked Mr. Cliff.

"We do have a few questions," said Dottie. "But not only about frogs."

"I'm just finishing up with a customer," said Mr. Cliff. "Can you wait for me in my office?"

"Yes," said the three friends together.

"It's a little crowded in there today," Mr. Cliff told them. "I got a big delivery this morning. And I think you'll find it interesting."

Mr. Cliff returned to his customer. Dottie, Casey, and Leon went into his office.

When they got there, they couldn't believe their eyes.

CHAPTER SEVEN

SPECIAL DELIVERY

Casey counted five tall tanks.

Dottie counted fifteen frogs.

Mr. Cliff finished with his customer and joined them.

"I see you found the delivery," he said. "The frogs came this morning, with a note."

He took the note out of his pocket and read it.

"Would you take care of these frogs and bring them to Fruitvale Park at noon on April first?"

"That's when the April Fool's Festival starts," said Leon.

"Is this a practical joke?" asked Casey.

"There's nothing funny about the frogs," said Mr. Cliff.

"They look like our frogs," said Leon.

"Where did you find yours?" asked Mr. Cliff.

"We were hunting for the gowk," Dottie explained.

"Hunting for the what?" asked Mr. Cliff.

"The missing gowk," Dottie said.

"Have you ever heard of a gowk?" asked Casey.

"No," Mr. Cliff admitted. He walked over to his bookshelf. He pulled out the biggest book and handed it to Dottie.

"This book lists lots of animals," he said. "Maybe you can look up what a gowk is."

Dottie, Casey, and Leon gathered around the book. The animals were listed in alphabetical order. Dottie turned to the page marked *G*.

"I see goose, gopher, and gorilla," she said. "But no gowk."

"I see grackle, grasshopper, and gray snake," said Leon. "But no gowk."

"Does this book list every animal there is?" asked Casey.

"Maybe not every one," said Mr. Cliff.

"I think we should try the library," Dottie said.

"That's a very good idea," said Mr. Cliff. "Miss Webster has even more books about animals than I do."

"Do you want to leave your frogs with me?" he asked. "I have an extra tank."

"Thanks," said Dottie. "Our frogs would be happier in a tank than in a library."

Dottie and Casey took the frogs out of the buckets. They put them in the empty tank.

Leon took the rocks out of the buckets. He put them in his pocket.

They thanked Mr. Cliff and hurried on.

They needed to get home before dark. And they didn't have much time.

CHAPTER EIGHT

IN THE BOOK BIN

They found the librarian, Miss Webster, near the reference books. She was pacing back and forth.

"Hi, Miss Webster," said Dottie.

"Do you have any books about gowks?" asked Casey.

"We have books about everything," said Miss Webster.

She was about to help them find what they wanted. But Officer Gill walked in.

"Thank goodness you're here," Miss Webster said to him. "I found them in the overnight book bin outside. Three of them!"

"Three gowks?" asked Casey.

"No," said Miss Webster. "Frogs. Can

you imagine? Three huge frogs in the book bin."

"What time did you find them?" asked Officer Gill.

They stepped inside Miss Webster's small office so she could explain what happened.

"I don't think Miss Webster is going to be able to help us today," said Dottie.

"Do you want to come back tomorrow?" asked Casey.

"Yes," said Leon. "But I want to look something up first."

Dottie and Casey followed Leon. He knew exactly where to find what he wanted. Leon pulled out a thick book from a shelf.

He put the book down on one of the long library tables. He turned to the page he wanted. Then he took a rock out of his pocket.

"Yes!" he said. "I thought so."

"What did you find?" asked Casey.

Leon pointed from the rock to the picture in the book. "It's Louisiana," he said.

"Were you looking for Louisiana?" asked Casey.

"No," said Leon. "But I'm really glad I found it."

"Why?" asked Casey.

"There's a city in Louisiana named Rayne," said Leon. "And it's known as the frog capital of the world!"

Leon knew lots of facts like that. Dottie and Casey were used to it.

The light flicked on and off.

"Closing time," called Miss Webster.

"Officer Gill has gone home," she said. "And it's time for you to go home, too."

Dottie, Casey, and Leon said good-bye to Miss Webster.

"How many states have you found so far?" Casey asked Leon as they left.

Leon didn't answer. He was staring at the rock in his hand.

"Is something wrong?" asked Casey.

Leon looked up.

"Sorry," he said. "I was just thinking about the frog capital of the world and the missing gowk."

"What does the frog capital of the world have to do with the missing gowk?" asked Casey.

"I feel like there's a connection," said Leon. "But I'm just not sure what it is."

He tried hard to think of it all the way home.

CHAPTER NINE

APRIL FOOL'S!

The next day was Saturday.

The Calendar Club agreed to meet in the clubhouse at eight-thirty.

Dottie got there first.

Casey and Leon arrived a minute later. Then they all got to work.

Dottie and Casey got ready for the look-alike contest.

Casey put Dottie's hair in braids so their hair would look the same.

Dottie gave Casey a notebook that looked exactly like the one she carried wherever she went.

"Do you like it?" Dottie asked. "Do you

want a different one? Do you need a pen or pencil?"

"Do I ask that many questions all the time?" asked Casey.

They all laughed.

"Come on outside," Leon said. "And watch me practice juggling eggs."

Casey and Dottie followed Leon outside.

He threw three eggs in the air. They fell to the ground and broke.

"Maybe you should try two at a time," said Dottie.

Leon took two eggs out of his pocket. He threw them in the air. They broke and splattered, too.

"I think you're going to win the look-alike contest," said Leon. "But I don't think I'm going to win the egg-juggling contest."

"Is it time to go?" asked Dottie. She turned to Casey. "Are you ready?"

"We have to check the Help Box first," Casey said. "It's Leon's turn."

Leon checked the box. "There's a note!" he said.

He read it out loud.

"Today is the day the gowk will be found.
Don't wander or dawdle on your way to town.
Get to the park and don't stop to talk.
The gowk will be watching wherever you walk.
Go have some April Fool's Festival fun.
And then at the end you will find out who won!"

"Let's go to the park," said Casey. "So we can be first."

She ran on ahead.

"What's so great about being first?" asked Dottie.

She and Leon laughed. Then they ran to catch up.

CHAPTER TEN

THE FESTIVAL BEGINS

They got to the park just before noon.

A large group of their classmates was already there. Everyone was talking about the missing gowk.

"We think it's a dog," said a boy named John. "We found red dog hair."

"We think it's a butterfly," said a girl named Ella. "We found a cocoon."

"We found five ladybugs," said a girl named Sallie. "Could a gowk could be a ladybug?"

A voice interrupted them. "Thank you for coming."

They all turned. It was Mr. Mac, the

owner of the new store. He stood on a small stage.

He smiled at the crowd. "Can everyone please take a seat?"

Everyone sat down on the folding chairs facing the stage.

"Welcome to the First-ever Fruitvale April Fool's Festival," said Mr. Mac. "Mrs. Mac and I have had a lot of fun planning this event. We hope you've had a lot of fun, too."

Mrs. Mac walked onto the stage. "Everyone is invited to stop by our store after the festival," she said. "We'll be open all day."

"She looks familiar," said Dottie.

Lizzy was sitting in front of them. She turned around. "She's my mom."

"That's why I recognized her!" said Dottie. "We met her with you."

"Is the new store yours?" asked Casey.

Lizzy nodded.

"Can you tell us the name of it?" asked Casey.

"I can tell you the address," said Lizzy. "It's Number Three Fruitvale Park Road."

"Number Three," said Casey. "Wasn't there a number three on one of the clues?"

"Can I have your attention?" called Mrs. Mac from the stage. "Do we have volunteers for the look-alike contest?"

Dottie and Casey raised their hands. Other people raised their hands, too.

Mrs. Mac invited them onto the stage.

"Will the judges please come up?" asked Mrs. Mac.

Lizzy ran up to the stage.

"Are you the judge?" asked Casey.

"I'm one of them," said Lizzy. "The other one's coming."

Dottie and Casey stared as another girl ran up to the stage.

They felt like they were seeing double. The girl looked exactly like Lizzy.

"I'm Kate," said the other judge.

"She's my sister," said Lizzy.

"We're twins," said Kate. "I'm the one you met looking at the sign for the festival."

"I'm the one who loves frogs and brownies," said Lizzy.

"We thought you were the same person," said Dottie.

"We're used to it," said Kate.

"It happens all the time," said Lizzy.

Dottie and Casey looked from one twin to the other.

"You look taller than Kate," Dottie said to Lizzy.

"She looks a whole inch taller," Casey said to Kate.

"Wow!" said Kate. "Hardly anyone notices that."

"Most people think we're exactly the same," said Lizzy. "You two would make great detectives."

Dottie and Casey smiled.

Then they lined up for their turn in the contest.

Mrs. Mac called out their names.

Dottie and Casey tried to walk exactly the same way. They held out their matching notebooks and pens as they walked. They stopped at the same time. They wrote in their notebooks. They put their notebooks in their back pockets. They tossed their braids behind their shoulders. Then they smiled their biggest smiles.

The crowd cheered.

There were other contestants. There was a mother and daughter look-alike. There was a brother and sister look-alike. There was even a man and his dog look-alike.

Finally, it was time to pick the winners.

Lizzy and Kate walked across the stage studying all the contestants.

"We pick Dottie," said Lizzy.

"And Casey," said Kate.

The crowd cheered again.

"Do we win a gowk?" asked Casey.

"We'll give out prizes later," said Mr. Mac. "But I have medals for you now."

Lizzy gave a medal to Dottie. Kate gave one to Casey.

"Now it's time for the egg-juggling contest," announced Mrs. Mac.

Casey, Dottie, Lizzy, and Kate sat down.

"I thought Leon was going to enter this contest," said Dottie.

Casey looked around. "Where is Leon?"

Leon was nowhere to be seen.

"Look," Dottie said to Casey. "Your mother is juggling eggs."

Casey looked at the stage. Her mother

was trying to juggle three eggs. She dropped them all and laughed. Everyone laughed with her.

"Did you know your uncle could juggle?" Casey asked.

Dottie looked. Her uncle Eddy was trying to juggle four eggs. He dropped them all, too. Everyone laughed some more.

"Anyone else?" asked Mr. Mac.

Warren Bunn and Derek Fleck ran up onto the stage. They threw eggs at each other.

Mrs. Bunn and Mrs. Fleck ran over and chased them back to their seats.

"We have two winners," said Mr. Mac. He gave medals to Mrs. Calendar and Uncle Eddy.

The crowd cheered.

"Does my mom win a gowk?" asked Casey.

"Does anyone know what a gowk is?" asked Mr. Mac.

People called out ideas. "A dog." "A butterfly." "A salamander." "A cat." "A hummingbird." "A fish."

"Dottie!" someone called. "Casey!"

Dottie and Casey turned. It was Leon.

They ran over to him. Leon whispered in their ears.

Dottie and Casey whispered in Leon's ears.

The three friends smiled at each other.

"I guess no one figured it out," Mr. Mac said to the crowd.

"Wait," Casey said.

"We figured it out," Leon added.

Dottie smiled. "We know where the missing gowk is!"

Everyone got quiet and waited.

The Calendar Club ran onto the stage to explain.

CHAPTER ELEVEN
FINDING THE GOWK

Dottie, Casey, and Leon stood next to Mr. and Mrs. Mac.

Leon held up a big book.

"It's in here," Leon told the crowd.

"That's not a gowk," Warren called out. "Why are you showing us a book?"

"Because I was thinking about a city in Louisiana called Rayne," Leon explained. "It's known as the frog capital of the world. That got me wondering if there was a gowk capital of the world. So I went to the library."

"What did you find there?" asked Mrs. Mac.

"This book," said Leon. "It's about

different traditions. And it talks about hunting for the gowk. That's a tradition in Scotland. You do it on April Fool's Day."

"You didn't find the gowk at all, did you?" asked Warren.

"That's the point," said Leon. "Hunting the gowk is like going on a wild goose chase. Everyone runs around looking for the gowk. But there is no gowk. You have lots of fun. But you can't ever find it."

"That's the way it usually works," said Dottie. "But today, we did find it."

"Where is it?" asked Derek. "I don't see it."

"Did you see the new store?" asked Casey. "Number Three Fruitvale Park Road?"

"The name of the store is a secret," said Dottie. "But we think we figured it out."

"Is the name of your store, The Missing Gowk?" Casey asked.

"Yes," said Mr. Mac. He smiled.

"It's a toy store," said Mrs. Mac. She smiled.

"We'll also have costumes on Halloween," said Kate.

"And a frog-jumping contest every April Fool's Day," said Lizzy.

"Is that where all the frogs came from?" asked Casey. "Your store?"

Kate and Lizzy nodded.

"That brings us to our last contest," said Mr. Mac. "Mr. Cliff, can you get the frogs?"

Dottie, Casey, and Leon helped Mr. Cliff get the frogs from his truck.

Everyone lined up to choose one.

Warren pushed to the front of the line. He took his sister with him.

"Emma," he said. "Pick the biggest one."

Soon everyone had a frog. Officer Gill blew his whistle. The frog-jumping contest began.

Warren's frog didn't move. It was too big.

Derek's frog jumped fast. But it went the wrong way.

Dottie's frog jumped far.

Leon's frog jumped farther.

Casey's frog jumped ahead of Leon's frog.

But Kate and Lizzy's frog jumped farthest of all.

The contest was over. Mr. and Mrs. Mac said everyone was a winner.

Then they handed out prizes from The Missing Gowk.

Dottie got a large stuffed bird with bright blue feathers.

"These feathers look just like the feather we found," said Dottie. "This must be where the first clue came from."

"You're right," said Lizzy.

Casey got a toy guitar. The strings were hard as wire.

"Is this where the second clue came

from?" she asked. "Is the fishing line really a guitar string?"

"Right again," said Kate.

Leon got a fake snake kit. It had wooden pieces that fit together to make a snake. The picture on the box showed a cobra with fangs.

"This must be where the snake fang came from!" Leon said.

"That's a relief," said Dottie. "I wasn't very happy thinking there was a snake with big fangs on the loose."

There was lots of laughter as everyone looked at their prizes.

Then Mr. Mac announced the festival was over.

"Thanks for coming," said Mrs. Mac.

Mr. Mac and Mr. Cliff invited Dottie, Casey, Leon, Lizzy, and Kate to come with them to release the frogs.

They went to the pond behind Fruitvale Elementary School and let the frogs go.

They watched them disappear behind trees, under leaves, and into the shallow water.

"I hope we get to go on another gowk hunt next year," said Leon.

Mr. Mac smiled. "I'm sure that can be arranged."

Then the three friends headed back to Daisy Lane.

They hadn't gotten far when voices called out behind them.

"Hey, Leon."

It was Warren and Derek, on their bikes.

"There's a giant woodpecker about to attack you," Warren yelled.

"It's going to peck your head if you don't run," yelled Derek.

Leon, Dottie, and Casey turned around. Their eyes got wide. They looked amazed.

"What is it?" asked Derek.

Leon pointed. "It's the frogs," he said. "We set them free behind the school."

"But they're coming back," said Dottie.

"Why do they look so mad?" asked Casey.

Warren started to pedal away as fast as he could.

"Wait for me," called Derek.

"April Fool's," called Leon.

Warren skidded to a stop. He turned and looked.

There weren't any frogs.

There was just Dottie, Casey, and Leon laughing.

"Made you look," said Leon.

And the three friends skipped all the way home.

The Monthly Calendar

~~~~~ Issue Seven • Volume Seven ~~~~~

APRIL

Publisher: Casey Calendar
Editor: Dottie Plum
Fact Checker: Leon Spector

Gowk Loose in Fruitvale!
Calendar Club to the Rescue!

The big news in Fruitvale this April was the First-ever Fruitvale April Fool's Festival. Posters all over town promised lots of fun events. They also promised that contest winners would win a gowk.

But what was a gowk? Before anyone could figure out what it was, the Calendar Club learned that a gowk was missing. All of Fruitvale joined in the hunt for the missing gowk. But it was Calendar Club members Casey Calendar, Dottie Plum, and Leon Spector who figured out what the missing gowk was and where it was hiding.

DOTTIE'S WEATHER BOX

Dottie woke up at 5:00 a.m. The temperature outside was 65 degrees. Dottie went back to sleep for three more hours. She woke up the second time at 8:00 a.m. The temperature outside was 75 degrees. How many degrees did the temperature go up?

ASK LEON

Do you have a question for Leon Spector? If you do, send it to him and he'll answer it for you. (Especially if it's about a state!)

Dear Leon,
Is there such a thing as a state frog?
From,
Croaking to Know

Dear Croaking,
There are lots of states that have state amphibians. Sometimes the state amphibian is a frog. Louisiana's state amphibian is the green tree frog. Missouri's is the North American bullfrog. If your state doesn't have a state amphibian, maybe your class can suggest one. Good luck!

Your friend,
Leon